Yu-Gi-Oh! GX

A New Hero

D1169018

SHONEN JUMP'S

Yu-Gi-Oh! GX

A New Hero

Adapted by Tracey West

SCHOLASTIC INC.
New York   Toronto   London   Auckland   Sydney
Mexico City   New Delhi   Hong Kong   Buenos Aires

No part of this work may be reproduced, stored in a retrieval system, or transmitted in any form or by any means, electronic, mechanical, photocopying, recording, or otherwise, without written permission of the publisher. For information regarding permission, write to Scholastic Inc., Attention: Permissions Department, 557 Broadway, New York, NY 10012.

ISBN-13: 978-0-439-88836-3
ISBN-10: 0-439-88836-0

© 2007 Kazuki Takahashi • NAS • TV TOKYO
© 1996 Kazuki Takahashi
© 2004 NAS • TV TOKYO

Published by Scholastic Inc.
SCHOLASTIC and associated logos are trademarks and/or registered trademarks of Scholastic Inc.

12 11 10 9 8 7 6 5 4 3 2 1   7 8 9 10 11 12/0

Printed in the U.S.A.
First printing, December 2007

◆ CHAPTER ONE ◆

GET YOUR REMATCH ON!

Jaden Yuki sat in a classroom at Duel Academy. For once, he wasn't taking a nap. He and some of the other students had gathered in the classroom to watch the big-screen TV. Aster Phoenix was giving a press conference.

Aster was one of the top professional duelists in the world. Jaden had already faced him in battle and won. But it wasn't a fair fight. Aster had dueled with a deck of random cards he had just bought. He lost to Jaden's impressive deck of Hero Monsters. That left Jaden wondering exactly what Aster was up to.

Now Aster was in the spotlight for winning the Duel Pro League match. He had beaten Zane Truesdale to do it. Zane was a star at Duel Academy. He had never lost a duel — not even to Jaden — until Aster came along.

Reporters crowded around Aster. They wanted to know what this dueling star would be doing next.

A female reporter shoved a microphone in front of Aster's face. "What an impressive win!" she said. "What's your secret?"

Aster looked into the camera with his big, blue eyes. The duelist wore his trademark white suit. His silvery hair framed his face.

"Like I tell my fans," Aster said, "winning duels is a piece of cake when destiny's got your back."

"Now tell us about this new deck of yours," the reporter said.

"Well, there's a reason I unveiled it today," Aster told her. "See, last week I paid a visit to Duel Academy. And get this — there's a student there who totally copied my deck!"

Jaden gasped in his seat. Aster had to be talking about *him!* But that was totally unfair. Jaden had been using a deck of Hero monsters for as long as he'd been dueling.

He hadn't copied Aster at all! If anything, Jaden had been surprised to see Aster use Hero monsters during his duel with Zane.

"I guess I can't blame him," Aster continued. "I mean, who wouldn't want to be like me?"

"Anyway, I had to reveal my deck before this wannabe student took all the credit," Aster went on. "You see, this student — who shall remain nameless — has sort of a following among hardcore dueling fans. And the last thing I need is some prep-school punk taking credit for my hard work!"

Jaden's friend Bastion Misawa sat in the seat behind Jaden. He leaned forward, frowning.

"That settles it," Bastion said. "I officially can't stand this guy."

Back on the TV screen, Aster continued bragging. "Now whether you like me or not, there's one fact out there that no one can dispute," he said. "I'm the best! I can't be beat! And to prove it, I'm challenging this schoolboy. I won't

tell you his name, but it rhymes with . . . Schmaden Schmuki!"

Jaden's friends gasped in shock.

"Hear me, Schmaden? You know who you are, card thief!" Aster cried. "You think your Aster rip-off deck is so great? Then prove it — by putting it up against *my* deck!"

Aster walked away from the reporters. Back in the classroom, Jaden's friends reacted to the surprise announcement.

"You already beat him once," pointed out Syrus Truesdale, Jaden's best friend.

Alexis Rhodes looked concerned. "But now he's got his *real* deck," she pointed out.

That didn't bother Jaden at all. He grinned. "This is just the challenge I've been looking for!" he said. "Time to get my rematch on!"

• CHAPTER TWO •

A THIEF IN THE NIGHT

Bastion and Syrus sat at the computer in Bastion's room. They watched pictures of Aster Phoenix on the screen. Aster surfing. Aster hang gliding. Aster skiing. Aster snowboarding . . .

"According to my research, there isn't a sport that Aster Phoenix hasn't mastered," Bastion announced. "And there's more. He has a high IQ as well as a photographic memory."

Syrus stared at the pictures. His blue eyes looked worried behind his glasses. "I have a photographic memory, too," he joked nervously. "Well, when I remember to load the film."

Jaden sat on Bastion's bed. He gave a loud yawn. Bastion and Syrus looked at him, surprised.

"Will you guys chill out?" Jaden said. "If you want to do some research, I have some homework that needs finishing. Otherwise, cool it with the spy mission."

"This is important!" Syrus told him. "Bastion's trying to pinpoint Aster Phoenix's weakness. And so far, there *is* none."

Jaden shook his head. "Syrus, you're my best bud. But you're taking all the fun out of this!"

He flopped back on the bed. "Ah, you gotta love these Ra Yellow beds," he said.

Then he started to snore.

On the docks of Academy Island, two men shivered in the wind. One was tall and thin; the other was short and fat. They both wore frilly blue uniforms.

"I'm freezing my croissants off!" complained Bonaparte, the short man. Bonaparte was the Vice Chancellor of the academy. He had a bald head, a brown mustache, and two beady eyes. "Where's Aster Phoenix already?"

Bonaparte was not a big fan of Jaden's — or of anyone else in the Slifer Red dorm. He couldn't wait to see Aster defeat him.

"All I know is I've lost all feeling below my chin," said the tall man, shivering. Vellian Crowler was the Chancellor of Duel Academy. He had a long nose and long, blond hair.

Crowler was anxious for Aster to arrive, too. He hoped Aster would become a student at the academy, bringing it fame and glory.

Both men stared over the dark ocean waters.
Where was Aster Phoenix?

Crowler and Bonaparte were looking in the wrong place. Aster wasn't arriving by boat.

Aster's private plane flew over Academy Island. He jumped out, a skyboard strapped to his feet. Aster surfed the wind and released his parachute at just the right time.

He landed on the roof of the Academy card shop. Aster was here to fulfill his destiny. Beating Jaden Yuki was just part of that.

The sound of breaking glass filled the night as a thief smashed the windows of the School Store. He emerged with packs of stolen cards in his hands.

Then a dark laugh filled the air. The thief stopped, startled.

"What's your rush, tough guy," Aster called down. "Now that you stole those cards, don't you want to use them?"

The thief looked back, confused. He looked on top of the card shop and gasped.

A sinister-looking Duel Monster stood there. His ragged red cape flapped against the night sky.

"What do you want?" the terrified thief asked.

Aster laughed darkly. "I'm just looking for a friendly duel!"

The strange monster descended from the roof.

The thief's scream shattered the quiet night.

◆ CHAPTER THREE ◆

ASTER'S JUSTICE

Jaden and his friends heard the scream from Bastion's dorm.

Crowler and Bonaparte heard it from the docks.

They all ran to the school store at the same time. Aster stood over the thief's fallen body, grinning.

"I have a little saying," he told the boy. "It goes: You just can't hide from destiny."

Then Aster threw the thief's cards on top of him. "You want free cards? Then take them. They won't be much use to you in prison!"

Crowler and Bonaparte reached Aster first.

"Halt! Who goes there?" Crowler called out.

Jaden ran up next, followed by Bastion and Syrus. Jaden skidded to a stop when he saw Aster.

"Aster Phoenix!" he said in surprise.

"Hey, who's that?" Syrus asked, pointing to the thief.

"Some punk who thought that crime paid off," Aster said smugly. "Turns out he was wrong."

Syrus knelt down by the boy's side. He looked like he had been tossed around in a storm. "Whoa, looks like you knocked him out cold."

"What have you done to him?" Bastion asked angrily.

Aster ignored Bastion. He chuckled and turned to Jaden. "So, how've you been, bro?"

Now Syrus was angry, too. "Hey, Bastion asked you a question!"

"Yeah, fess up," Jaden added.

"Hey, save it for the duel," Aster said coolly.

Bonaparte rushed up to him. "Bonjour, Monsieur Phoenix! Welcome to our school. I'm Chancellor Bonaparte, and this here is my personal assistant," he said, nodding to Crowler.

Crowler scowled at the outrageous lie.

"Sorry, but I'm not supposed to talk to management," Aster said. "All business goes through my agent."

"Your agent?" Bonaparte asked.

"Yeah, guys like me don't have time to deal with the little people," Aster replied. He walked toward Jaden now, leaving the stunned men behind him.

"I'll see you bright and early for your duel," Aster told Jaden. "By the way, other than your friends here, there are no spectators allowed. I'm a pro. People pay money to watch me duel. No way am I giving a free show to a bunch of amateurs."

Jaden was starting to like Aster less and less every minute. "Come on, man, that's not cool. A lot of students here look up to you. And you're gonna tell them you can't come? Give me a break! How selfish can you be?"

Aster laughed. "Are you for real? You've got a lot to learn about the business," he said.

Then he walked off into the night.

"Hey, wait! Where can we find this agent of yours?" Bonaparte called after him.

"We've got business to discuss!" Crowler cried. He and Bonaparte ran off after Aster.

Jaden watched them leave. His brown eyes gleamed with anticipation.

He couldn't wait to face Aster on the field again!

Jaden arrived at the arena the next morning. The stands were empty, except for a few students.

Syrus and Bastion were there. Alexis came with her friends Mindy and Jasmine from the Obelisk Blue dorm. Chazz Princeton was there, too. He was once one of Jaden's rivals, but circumstances had put them on the same team more than once.

Hassleberry was there, too. Jaden had defeated the dino-obsessed duelist. Now Hassleberry was a loyal friend.

Jaden's friends watched from the stands as he walked out into the arena.

"They're about to start," Alexis said nervously.

"Yer backup troops are right here, sarge!" Hassleberry called out.

"Good luck!" Syrus added.

Jaden looked down at his Duel Disk. His cards were inside, just waiting to be called on.

"Come on boys," he whispered to them. "We can do this."

The sound of cheering caused Jaden to look up.

"We love Aster, yes we do. We love Aster, how about you!"

Mindy and Jasmine had moved to Aster's side of the arena. They waved to Aster, hoping to get his attention.

"How pathetic," Alexis said, frowning.

"Yeah, they're supposed to be with us," Syrus said.

Alexis stood up. "I'm gonna have a word with those two!"

Hassleberry put his arm in front of her. "Oh, no you don't!"

"We're not falling for that," Syrus said. "You just want to sit near Aster!"

Alexis blushed.

"All right," Bonaparte announced into the micro-phone. "Help me welcome Aster Phoenix! The biggest star of our time!"

"With an *ego* to match," Crowler muttered.

Jaden turned back to his deck. The spirit of the Winged Kuriboh card flew out. Jaden and the card had a special bond.

Winged Kuriboh was a brown, fuzzy creature with big eyes and wings. Now its big eyes were filled with worry.

"What's up pal?" Jaden asked.

Winged Kuriboh gave a concerned squeak.

"I won't let my guard down. Don't worry," Jaden told him. "I know this guy's supposed to be the best. But

we beat him once, and we can do it again. Trust me, it's all good."

Winged Kuriboh squeaked again in reply. It didn't look reassured at all. It disappeared into the deck.

Aster sized up Jaden from across the field. "I'll show him what a deck of *real* heroes can do," he said confidently.

"All right!" Jaden called out. "Time to loosen your tie, roll up your sleeves, and get your game on!"

"Please, I won't even break a sweat," Aster said calmly. "You're going down, man."

"Well, there's only one way to find out," Jaden replied, looking his opponent squarely in the eye.

Jaden and Aster activated their Duel Disks.

"Let's do this!" both boys cried out.

⟨ • CHAPTER FOUR • ⟩

HERO VS. HERO

Both duelists started off with 4000 attack points.

"*I'll* kick things off," Aster said. "Check this out. Look familiar?"

Aster held up a card. A Hero monster appeared on the field. He had a sturdy gray body with thick arms and legs, and 2000 defense points.

"It's Elemental Hero Clayman!" Aster announced. He played the Hero in defense mode. Then he ended his turn.

"I'll let you off the hook for now," Aster said.

"How strange," Bastion observed from the sidelines. "Now Jaden has to fight *against* some of his favorite monsters."

Jaden was up for the challenge. "Pretty sweet opening move," he admitted. "But watch this!"

Jaden drew his first cards. He grinned. "Hey, not bad. I activate Polymerization!"

"Yes! It's time for some fusion action!" Syrus cheered.

Hassleberry nodded. "Now he can order a higher ranking monster to the field."

Jaden set the card's magic in motion. "Now I fuse Avian with Burstinatrix," he said, holding up two Hero cards. "So Elemental Hero Flame Wingman, come on down!"

The two Heroes fused together to form a massive Hero. One of its arms ended in a dragon's head. The other was a shining white wing. Flame Wingman had 2100 attack points.

"And now, Flame Wingman attack!" Jaden yelled. "Infernal Rage!"

Flame Wingman extended his arm and a wave of fiery flames shot from the dragon's mouth. The flames engulfed Clayman. The big hero shattered. Aster winced to see his monster destroyed.

"And that's not all," Jaden went on. "Thanks to Wingman's super power, your Clayman's attack points come out of your *life* points! Take it away, Wingman!"

Aster watched, frustrated, as his life points dropped down to 3200.

Chazz nodded in the stands. "What do you know? Seems the pro took the first blow."

"Lucky shot. But that'll change," Aster said. It was his turn now. He drew a card and smiled.

"Guess what I just drew?" he asked.

"How should I know?" Jaden shot back.

"Simple. You just played the same thing," Aster said, grinning. "Polymerization!"

Jaden's friends gasped.

"Oh please," Bastion said, rolling his eyes. "Try playing something original!"

Now Aster held up two Hero cards. "Just like you, I fuse my Avian with my Burstinatrix," he said. "But unlike you, I'm forming Elemental Hero Phoenix Enforcer!"

The new Hero appeared on the field. He was red and green, like Elemental Hero Flame Wingman. He also had 2100 attack points. But his right arm was a huge dragon claw.

Jaden was psyched. "I was hoping to see him! This is so cool!"

"Is that so?" Aster replied. "Well, how's this for cool?"

Phoenix Enforcer launched an attack. A swirling

burst of rainbow light shot from the dragon claw. It raced across the field.

Flame Wingman responded with another ball of flame. The two attacks met in the middle of the field. The rainbow blast shattered Jaden's Hero, but Phoenix Enforcer was still standing. Jaden gasped in surprise.

"Wait! That should have been a draw!" Hassleberry cried.

"One small technicality," Bastion said. "His Phoenix Enforcer can't be destroyed in battle."

Jaden nodded, impressed. "Way to one-up me."

"What did you expect? Our decks are similar, not equal," Aster told him. "Think of the cards we use as a mirror. They reflect who we are, and what motivates our actions."

"Do you have to get so deep?" Jaden complained.

"I rest my case," Aster replied. "The point is, my deck's better!"

Jaden raised an eyebrow. "Oh, yeah? We'll see about that! I summon Elemental Hero Bubbleman!"

Elemental Hero Bubbleman had a blue uniform and a long, white cape. Water hoses snaked across his body. He had 800 attack points.

"Since it's the only card on my field, its special effect kicks in," Jaden said, "allowing me to draw two cards from my deck. And next I'll play . . . the Warrior Returning Alive spell card!"

Jaden held up the card. "So if you don't mind, I'll be bringing a warrior back from my graveyard . . . my Elemental Hero Avian, to be exact. And then I'll fuse him together with my Bubbleman and my Sparkman to form . . . drumroll please . . . Elemental Hero Tempest!"

Elemental Hero Tempest had huge white wings, clawed feet, and a mask over the top of his face. Fused from three heroes, he had 2800 attack points.

"Now attack with Glider Strike!" Jaden yelled.

Tempest shot a powerful water blast from the water gun on his right arm. The water jet pounded Elemental Hero Phoenix Enforcer. Aster's life points dropped down to 2500.

Alexis grinned. "Aster's monster may be invincible, but the same thing can't be said for his life points."

"Don't start celebrating just yet," Bastion said cautiously. "This duel has quite a ways to go."

"Back to me!" Aster said, drawing a card. "Well, whaddya know. Here's a card I haven't seen in a while. Polymerization!"

Syrus sighed. "Aw, man. That's only fun when Jaden plays it."

"I take one part Phoenix Enforcer and add a pinch of Sparkman," Aster said. "And out comes Elemental Hero Shining Phoenix Enforcer!"

The new hero had armor of shining silver metal. Jaden was really excited to see Aster using different Hero monsters. This one had 2500 attack points.

"And thanks to his special ability, he gains 300 attack points for every Hero monster in my graveyard!" Aster said.

Elemental Hero Phoenix Enforcer's attack points rose to a serious 4000.

"That's a whole lotta Hero," Jaden had to admit.

Hassleberry shook his head. "That bad boy's gonna be all over Jaden like flies on a cow pie."

"You're way out of your league!" Aster called out to Jaden, his blue eyes gleaming. "Shining Phoenix go! Attack with Shimmer Kick!"

Elemental Hero Phoenix Enforcer leaped into the air. He flipped completely, then lunged at Elemental Hero Tempest. He landed a fierce blow to Tempest's chest.

Jaden's Hero was defeated!

◄ CHAPTER FIVE ►

IT'S D-TIME!

Jaden's life points took the rest of the damage. He braced himself as they dropped down to 2800 points.

"That'll do," Aster said. "So I'll put down a facedown and call it a turn."

"Not too bad," Jaden said. It took a lot more than losing some life points to get him down. "But get this! I activate Pot of Greed. So now I can draw two cards."

Jaden did just that. He smiled when he saw them. "Sweet! And next, I'll activate Miracle Fusion!"

The card in Jaden's hand had a letter "H" emblazoned over two swirling heroes. "Here's how it works," Jaden explained. "First, I remove any fusion-material monsters from the field or my graveyard. Then I can summon something stronger. So here goes! I combine my Flame Wingman and Elemental Hero Sparkman to form this!"

Jaden put the new card on his Duel Disk. A Hero monster appeared on the field: Elemental Hero Shining Flare Wingman. Sharp, white blades extended from each arm.

"And if you think he's strong now, just wait till he gains 1200 points, thanks to the heroes in my graveyard," Jaden said. He grinned as Elemental Hero Shining Flare Wingman's attack points jumped up to 3700.

"Are you done?" Aster asked. "I was hoping after that big production that you'd play a monster that can actually accomplish something. But no. You spent twenty minutes summoning a monster that's *weaker* than mine."

"Not exactly," Jaden replied. He loved moments like this. "You see, attack points aren't everything. So if you don't mind, I'll continue . . . by playing Light Laser!"

The card Jaden held up showed a black gadget shaped like a half-moon. The gadget appeared on Shining Flare Wingman's hand. A blue laser beam shot out from it.

"Now when my Shining Wingman attacks, your hero is automatically removed from play!" Jaden announced.

Chazz nodded in the stands. "Not bad, slacker. Not bad at all."

"Jaden's got the upper hand," Bastion agreed. "What would Aster's fans think? It's no wonder he insisted the arena be empty."

And Jaden still had more cards to throw out.

"Next I play a Field Spell. It's called Skyscraper," Jaden said. "I figured we could use a change of scenery."

When Jaden played the card, the dueling field transformed into a city. Tall buildings rose up all around them — the perfect habitat for Heroes.

"Oh, and it boosts my Wingman by a thousand points!" Jaden added.

Now Shining Wingman had 4700 attack points — 700 more than Phoenix Enforcer.

"And now, Shining Flare Wingman, attack!" Jaden yelled.

Jaden's Hero flew up above the skyscrapers. His laser light lit up the field.

"All right, fine," Aster said. "We'll go out with a bang!"

He sent Shining Phoenix Enforcer up to face Shining Flare Wingman. The two heroes faced each other against the city skyline.

"Wingman, activate Light Laser!" Jaden ordered.

Shining Flare Wingman lifted the blue laser beam, then brought it down over Shining Phoenix Enforcer's chest.

There was a small explosion as Shining Phoenix Enforcer shattered. Aster's life points dropped down to 1800.

Jaden's friends were impressed by the move.

"Awesome! Who's the pro duelist now?" Alexis said.

"Jaden!" Syrus cheered.

Elemental Hero Shining Flare Wingman flew back to Jaden's side.

"This is what I call a sweet duel," Jaden said. "What could be better? Hero monsters going head to head? It's so chill!"

Aster looked supremely annoyed now. "What's with you? You think this is all just a big joke?" he cried out angrily. "Well I've got news for you, joy-boy. Dueling isn't about having fun. At least not for me. But someone like you would never understand that. I duel for justice. And revenge. Aw, forget it . . ."

His voice trailed off. He knew Jaden wouldn't understand.

"It's too late for that now," Jaden said.

"I chose my Hero cards for a reason," Aster told him, his blue eyes glaring at Jaden. "And punks like you who use them just 'cause you think they look cool make me sick!"

"Chill out," Jaden said. Aster had it all wrong. Jaden had total respect for his Elemental Heros.

"Look, these cards are my life! They're everything to me," Aster said, his voice pained. "So *you* chill out."

Jaden shrugged. "I'm always chill."

Aster shook his head. "Whatever. I told you I wouldn't get it. I was destined to build this deck, and here's proof. I activate my D-Time card!"

Aster's facedown card flipped up. It had a picture of a cup of tea with a letter "D" floating inside. Jaden had never seen it before.

"So thank you," Aster said. "You triggered this trap when you destroyed my Phoenix Enforcer. When it leaves the field, I can unleash a new breed of Heroes from my deck. They're known as the Destiny Heroes!"

"Destiny Heroes?" Jaden asked. He *definitely* hadn't heard of those before.

"What heroes?" Chazz repeated.

"Destiny, son," Hassleberry informed him. "They already said it twice."

"What are they?" Syrus wondered.

Everyone turned to Bastion. He was an expert on just about every Duel Monsters card.

Bastion shrugged. "Don't look at me."

"You don't know?" Syrus asked, worried. That couldn't be good. Who knew what kind of power the new cards had?

"It's time to open your eyes to the true power of the Elemental Heroes!" Aster cried.

"Enough with the dramatic speeches, bro!" Jaden said.

"Well fine," Aster said. "Then I won't tell you my secret. Unless of course, you want to know the truth."

Jaden took the bait. "What truth?" he asked.

"The truth about a secret series of Hero monsters created by Industrial Illusions but never released to the public," Aster told him. "It's known as the D-series. But why don't I just show you?"

Aster placed a card into his Duel Disk.

"First, I'll play my Clock Tower Prison field spell!" Aster announced. The skyscrapers exploded as Aster's field spell took over. A long, concrete building topped by a stone clock tower appeared.

With Skyscraper gone, Elemental Hero Flare Wingman's attack points dropped back down to 3700.

"This clock is the key ingredient," Aster said.

"It is? But why?" Jaden asked.

"Oh, so now you want to hear my speech," Aster said lightly. "Why don't we just say that with every tick of this clock . . . I come closer to victory!"

Aster looked up at the clock tower. He raised his arm dramatically. "Now, hands of fate, turn! And usher in the doom!"

Dark clouds quickly gathered behind the clock tower. A cold wind blew. The hands of the clocks spun around and around. When the hands hit midnight, a Hero monster appeared on top of the clock tower.

It was the same creepy-looking hero Aster had used when he dueled the thief. His tattered red cape blew in the wind. The top of his head was bald and white. Two blood red eyes peered out from over a red collar. A blue gem gleamed in his forehead. Both of his hands ended in long, sharp claws. A small skull clasped the monster's cape around his neck.

"What *is* that thing?" Syrus asked, horrified. The monster looked more evil than heroic.

"Jaden, meet Destiny Hero - Doom Lord!" Aster shouted. Doom Lord swooped down from the clock tower and stood by Aster's side.

Jaden wasn't scared by the monster's looks. He wasn't impressed by Doom Lord's attack points either — a measly 600.

"No offense, but he seems weak," Jaden said.

"Let's test that theory," Aster said. "Doom Lord, show him what you've got!"

Chazz shook his head. "That was dumb."

"I concur, Chazz," Bastion said. "Why would Aster activate that? He clearly has the weaker monster."

Aster grinned. "Oh yeah? Did I mention his ability?"

Aster pointed at his monster. "Now Destiny Hero - Doom Lord! Send him packing with Impending Doom Grip!"

Destiny Hero - Doom Lord struck at Shining Flare Wingman with a clawed hand. The attack shouldn't have done any damage at all to the stronger monster.

But Aster was still smiling. "See ya. In the future, that is."

Elemental Hero Shining Flare Wingman vanished before Jaden's eyes.

"Hey, what did you do to my Wingman?" Jaden cried. "He's gone!"

"Yeah, but not for long," Aster replied. "You see, each turn my Doom Lord can send one of your monsters two turns into the future."

Jaden shook his head. "That doesn't even make sense."

"To you. 'Cause you've got a lot to learn about destiny," Aster said scornfully. "And unfortunately for you, right now, I'm controlling yours. And your future's looking pretty grim!"

• CHAPTER SIX •

DAWN OF THE DESTINY HEROES

When things get tough in a duel, some duelists just give up. Others get nervous. Others get angry.

Jaden Yuki gets really excited.

"You think things are intense now?" Jaden asked. "Well, just wait! It's my move."

"Whoa, chill out," Aster said, grinning like he knew a secret. "Don't you know what time it is? Time to get a new watch! But don't worry, I happen to have a clock. And it's clicking toward your defeat!"

Everyone looked up at the clock tower. The hands spun around quickly, stopping only at each hour mark.

"What's the deal?" Alexis wondered aloud.

"Confused? Wondering why I put a giant clock on the

field?" Aster teased. "Well, I wouldn't want to ruin the suspense for you. So you'll have to wait."

Jaden shrugged. "That's cool. 'Cause whatever that thing does, I'm pretty sure I've got the cards in my deck to stop it."

"Wrong," Aster shot back. "No one can stop the hands of fate!"

Jaden shook his head. Aster was way obsessed with this whole destiny thing.

"Don't be so sure," Jaden told him. "I summon Wroughtweiller in attack mode!"

A tough-looking metal dog appeared on the field. He had 800 attack points.

"Now sic 'em, boy!" Jaden yelled.

Wroughtweiller jumped across the field and slammed into Destiny Hero - Doom Lord. Aster's monster didn't have enough points to withstand the attack. He shattered. Aster grimaced as his life points dropped down to 1600.

Then his expression changed to a grin. "Thanks for the help!" he said. "Now I can play this!"

Aster's facedown card flipped up. It showed a picture of a spotlight. There was a letter "D" in the center of the light. The spotlight turned on, projecting a big letter "D" in the dark sky above.

"It's my Destiny Signal!" Aster announced.

"Destiny again? That's real original," Jaden joked.

"I heard that!" Aster snapped. "You're just bitter that I have the upper hand. Well I can't say that I blame you. 'Cause after all, if you hadn't triggered my trap card, I wouldn't be able to summon a new Destiny Hero from the field!"

Aster triumphantly held up a new card in his hand. A big cocoon made of green metal appeared. The cocoon opened to reveal a Hero monster. He had wild red hair, green armor on his legs, and a metal green wing strapped to each arm. He had 800 attack points.

"Meet Destiny Hero - Captain Tenacious!" Aster cried. "And that's not all. Now that the introductions are out of the way, the captain can demonstrate his hidden talent. Hit it!"

"Talent? What's he gonna do, play the kazoo?" Jaden quipped.

"Go ahead. Make jokes," Aster said. "But believe me, I'll have the last laugh. Now Captain, show time! Let's give this amateur a taste of what you can really do!"

A bright light flashed, and Doom Lord appeared on the field once again.

"Hey, that's Doom Lord!" Hassleberry said, surprised. "What's going on, Bastion?"

"Scientifically speaking, Jaden's getting his bum
kicked!" Bastion remarked.

Back on the field, Aster was toying with Jaden.
"What to do? Oh, here's an idea," he said. "I'll summon
another Destiny Hero. Meet Diamond Dude!"

Destiny Hero - Diamond Dude appeared, with 1400
attack points flashing next to him. He had shining white hair
and wore a black uniform and green cape. The mask over
his eyes shone like glass. Super-sharp diamonds jutted from

his shoulders and legs. He even had pointed diamonds on
the ends of his arms.

"Like his friends, Diamond Dude's got a talent," Aster
bragged. "He likes to play card tricks. So I'll flip a card, and
if it happens to be a spell, it goes straight to the graveyard
until my next turn!"

Jaden raised an eyebrow. This duel was getting more interesting by the minute.

Aster drew a card from his disk. "Well, would you look at that," he said. "It's my Misfortune spell card. And how appropriate. Because now, Misfortune's in your future!"

• CHAPTER SEVEN •

TIME TO GET SERIOUS!

"Now who should I sic on you next?" Aster pondered out loud. "I know. My Diamond Dude!"

Destiny Hero - Diamond Dude charged across the field at Wroughtweiller. Sizzling lightning shot from his right hand. The attack destroyed Wroughtweiller. Jaden's life points dropped down to 2200.

Jaden recovered quickly. He grinned at Aster. "This time you helped *me*. 'Cause when Wroughtweiller's destroyed, his ability activates! And I get back an Elemental Hero *plus* Polymerization!"

The two cards shot out of Jaden's Duel Disk. But it was still Aster's turn.

"Is this supposed to *scare* me or something?" Aster

asked. "Sorry. Not gonna happen. Now Captain Tenacious. Attack him directly!"

Destiny Hero - Captain Tenacious flew across the field. He slammed into Jaden with the metal wing attached to his right hand. Jaden flew back against the floor of the field. His life points dropped down to 1400.

Jaden struggled to sit up. Aster looked happy to see his opponent down.

"I'll place this little number facedown and then call it a turn," Aster said.

Jaden strained to get to his feet.

"It's about time," Jaden said. He was happy to see some new monsters on the field.

"Speaking of time, it sure does fly when you're having fun!" Aster said, looking up at the big clock. The clock's hands kept spinning and spinning. "Too bad time's on my side today!"

Syrus sighed. "Enough with the clock references!"

It was Jaden's turn now. He had some of his own strategy planned.

"Alrighty, *time* to summon my Bubbleman!" he said, getting into the spirit. "And just wait till he *clocks* you. See? I can make witty puns, too!"

Jaden drew two cards from his Duel Disk. "Anyway, now I can draw two new cards, thanks to Bubbleman's special effect. Then I play this!"

Jaden held up a card with a picture of a massive water gun on it.

"Bubble Blaster, which doubles my hero's strength!" Jaden said. As he spoke, Bubbleman's attack points rose to 1600. "Now Bubbleman, attack with Bombarding Bubble Barrage!"

Elemental Hero Bubbleman pointed the Water Gun at Captain Tenacious. A forceful spray of water streamed across the field.

"Sorry to burst your bubble!" Aster said. "But it's trap time! Go, D-Shield!"

Aster's trap card flipped up on the field. Destiny Hero - Captain Tenacious raised his metal wings in front of him like a shield. They deflected Bubbleman's attack. Tenacious didn't take any damage at all. He flipped over into defense mode automatically — that was the power of the shield.

"D-Shield. My Heroes never leave home without it. And now you can see why," Aster bragged. "'Cause now Captain Tenacious can't be destroyed in battle!"

It was hard not to be impressed by Aster's move.

"He may be annoying, but he's good," Chazz pointed out.

"Aster took a monster that resurrects other monsters and made it invincible!" Crowler said.

Bonaparte nodded. "Guess that's why they pay him the big bucks!"

"Why don't you let me take it from here?" Aster said.

"Wait a sec!" Jaden called out. "Since two turns have passed, I get my Wingman back!"

Elemental Hero Shining Flare Wingman appeared back on the field. His polished armor gleamed.

"Congratulations," Aster said dryly. "But if you remember, I get a card back, too. The one in my graveyard. My Misfortune. Or should I say *your* misfortune."

Jaden braced himself for what was coming next. Any card called Misfortune couldn't mean good news!

"When my Battle Phase skips, half the attack points of one of *your* monsters comes right out of your life points. And I chose your Wingman!" Aster revealed.

Jaden watched helplessly, as Shining Flare Wingman sent an attack of shining light across the field. A protective bubble rose up around Aster. The light reflected back across the field — slamming into Jaden! He groaned as his life points dropped to 150.

Jaden struggled to make sense of what was happening. He could deal with losing life points. But not having control of his Hero — that was something else.

"You turned him against me!" Jaden said angrily.

"That was low," Alexis said.

"No joke!" Syrus and Hassleberry agreed.

"There's more," Aster went on. "Remember my Doom Lord? Well he's about to cut your little reunion short. By sending your Shining Flare Wingman packing!"

Destiny Hero - Doom Lord raced across the field and touched Elemental Hero Wingman with a long, clawed hand. Once again, Shining Flare Wingman disappeared.

"Don't worry. He's not going far," Aster said. "Just two turns into the future!"

"Again?" Jaden cried. A bead of sweat rolled down his face. Aster's strategies were pretty sweet. He'd have to think fast to counter them.

"Poor Jaden," Alexis said. "Thanks to Aster's Destiny cards he's lost control of his own monsters. I've never seen him like this."

"This duel is remarkable," Bastion remarked. "It breaks down every known formula. Jaden can't make a choice because all of his moves have been pre-determined!"

CHAPTER EIGHT

ELEMENTAL HERO NECROID SHAMAN!

"Let's try this again, shall we?" Jaden asked. He was ready to deal out some serious damage to Aster.

"Ah, ah, ah," Aster said. "How many times are you going to forget the nine-story clock towering above your head?"

Jaden looked up at the clock. The hands spun around quickly once again. They landed on the nine o'clock hour. The clock chimed loudly nine times.

"It's nine o'clock," Aster said. "The countdown to your defeat is almost over!"

Jaden frowned, frustrated. What was Aster talking about? He didn't want to let this guy get to him.

"You hear that bell, don't you? Well, it tolls for you!"

Aster cried out. "I said you were destined to lose. *Now* do you believe in destiny?"

Jaden chuckled.

"What's wrong?" Aster asked. "Pressure getting to you?"

"You kidding?" Jaden replied. "Guys like me live for pressure. It keeps me at the top of my game. Anyway, I've been looking for a serious challenge ever since the semester started. Plus with all these new Destiny Heroes of yours, I'm picking up some *sweet* strategies!"

Aster shook his head. "Dude, you gotta get out more," he said.

"And besides, you could never handle a deck like mine. So stick to your *own* heroes. My Destiny Heroes are the rockinest dudes in the game. They're way out of your league!"

"Gimme a break," Jaden said. Aster's whole attitude

was really annoying. "I mean sure they're cool and all, but I wouldn't call them the 'best in the game.'"

Aster's eyes flashed with anger. "I'd watch what I said if I were you," he warned.

"All right," Jaden replied. "I'll watch myself . . . say this! Bombarding Bubble Barrage!"

Bubbleman launched an attack at Destiny Hero - Doom Lord. A forceful spray of water bombarded Doom Lord. The Destiny Hero vanished from the field once again. Aster's life points dipped to 600.

In the stands, Jaden's friends cheered.

"See ya!" Syrus yelled.

"Yowzer!" Hassleberry exclaimed. "Now that was a good ol' fashioned hind whoopin'!"

"Think that was tough? Well just wait till my Captain's special ability kicks in," Aster threatened.

Jaden didn't care how many times Captain Tenacious brought back Doom Lord. He planned to be finished with Aster long before then.

"Big deal," Jaden countered. "I play Clayman!"

Jaden played his massive gray Hero in defense mode. Clayman's 2000 defense points could withstand almost any attack.

"Now give me your best shot!" Jaden said confidently.

"If you insist," Aster said. "Captain, time to do your thing. Bring back our old pal Doom Lord!"

Doom Lord reappeared on the field. Aster nodded with satisfaction.

"Diamond Dude! Time for your special effect, my man," Aster went on. He took a card from his deck and looked at it. "Since I just flipped over a spell card, I can use it next turn once I store it in my graveyard. And in the meantime, Doom Lord, strut your stuff! Float that bubble boy into the future!"

Doom Lord flew across the field. He sent Elemental Hero Bubbleman away with one swipe of his clawed hand.

"See ya in two turns," Aster said snidely. "Next, I'll hook up Captain Tenacious with Ring of Magnetism. Of course, like most bling bling it comes with a price. The ring bearer has to give up a few points."

A ring of green, glowing light encircled Destiny Hero - Captain Tenacious. Aster's life points dropped down to 300. But he didn't seem worried at all.

"The upside is, you're only allowed to attack the monster that's wearing the ring," Aster told Jaden.

Jaden tried to hold back his frustration. First, Aster turned his own monster against him. Now he was deciding who Jaden could attack.

"Now Jaden's forced to attack a monster that's invincible," Bastion remarked.

"What's his problem?" Alexis wondered. "Let Jaden duel!"

Aster smirked at Jaden. "What's wrong? Feel like you've lost control?"

"Not quite," Jaden said. He held up the cards in his hand. It was his turn. Aster could control a lot of things, but he couldn't control Jaden's strategy. He could get out of this yet.

"Sorry, bro, but I call the shots!" Aster called out. "And my *time* has arrived!"

The giant clock hit the stroke of midnight. It chimed twelve times. A gloomy sound rang through the arena. Bonaparte and Crowler shrieked in alarm.

Hmm, Jaden thought. *I don't know what that clock's about, but I better act fast!*

He held up a card. "Here goes something!" he yelled. "It's fusion time! So I'll combine my Elemental Hero Wildheart with my Necroshade, in order to create my newest hero."

Jaden's two heroes swirled until they fused together. A new Hero stood on the field next to Jaden. He was larger than both heroes. He had Wildheart's muscled body. Tribal marks were painted on his chest and shoulders. His long, flowing hair was the same bright red as Necroshade's armor. The new Hero boasted 1900 attack points.

"Give it up for Elemental Hero Necroid Shaman!" Jaden cried, pumping his fist in the air.

Aster just giggled. "You really call that freak a hero? Sorry dude. But that thing doesn't even register on the Hero scale."

"Don't you want to hear his special ability?" Jaden asked.

"No," Aster said flatly.

"Well, I'm going to tell you anyway," Jaden replied cheerfully. "I get to sacrifice a monster from *your* side of the field. Then I can summon a replacement monster from your graveyard! So good-bye Captain Tenacious and hello Mister Avian!"

Jaden grinned as Destiny Hero - Tenacious vanished, along with the Ring of Magnetism. Now Jaden could attack whichever monster he wanted. Elemental Hero Avian appeared in the Captain's place.

Jaden was one move away from winning the match. All he had to do was get rid of Destiny Hero - Doom Lord, and Aster would take the rest of the damage. His life points would drop to zero.

Jaden's friends saw what was coming.

"Thatta boy! Excellent maneuver there, soldier," Hassleberry cheered.

"Ditto!" Syrus called out. "Now kick him to the curb, Academy style!"

"Well said, Syrus," Alexis agreed. "Finish him off, Jay!"

◆ CHAPTER NINE ◆

ASTER IN CONTROL

Elemental Hero Necroid Shaman jumped across the field. He struck Doom Lord with his long staff. Doom Lord shattered and vanished in a cloud of dust.

The dust cleared. But instead of Aster's fallen form, Jaden saw Aster standing tall, smiling.

Jaden was confused. "Huh?"

"Well, well, well," Aster said. "Looks like I'm still standing. I wonder if it has something to do with this clock. You know the one I've been talking about for the past eleven minutes? It's about time I told you what it does. As long as it's here, I can't lose a single life point. I'm invincible!"

"Oh man," Jaden said. "I can't say I was expecting that. I'll throw two facedowns and call it a turn."

Jaden placed his facedown cards. He was disappointed, but not down.

Chazz couldn't believe it. "All these monsters and Jaden gets his butt kicked by a clock?"

Bastion shook his head. "No, it's much worse. You see, Chazz, Aster's learned to control time itself!"

Aster was clearly enjoying himself on the field. "Take a look. Here comes a blast from your past!"

Jaden's Elemental Hero Shining Flare Wingman appeared back on the field.

Bastion nodded. "Now I understand. Aster believes everything is predetermined."

"So he controls every part of the duel," Alexis said. "Whoa, that's pretty deep."

"Here comes something else from the past," Aster went on. "Magical Stone Excavation!"

Aster's spell card reappeared. It showed a cluster of shining purple crystals.

"So now I toss out two cards and a spell card returns from my graveyard," Aster went on. "Which one? You remember my Misfortune card, don't you? I choose a monster of yours. And then half of its original attack points come right out of your life points."

Jaden grimaced. He knew what was coming. Aster was going to choose the monster with the most life points.

"Shining Flare Wingman! Take Jaden down!" Aster yelled.

Shining Flare Wingman's white blast careened across the field. It bounced right off of Aster, then headed back across the field. . . .

"Jaden, no!" yelled Syrus and Hassleberry. They knew that once Jaden got hit, he'd lose the duel. He didn't have enough life points left to withstand the attack.

Jaden just smiled. "You are so predictable," he told Aster. "I play my De-Fusion and Burial from a Different Dimension!"

The two trap cards in front of Jaden flipped up at the same time.

"*Now* who's in charge?" Jaden asked. "First, I can take any monster that's traveled through time and send it to my graveyard. But not before I defuse it to get back to Sparkman and Flame Wingman!"

Jaden's trap cards worked together. First, Elemental Hero Shining Flare Wingman defused into the two Heroes it was made up of. Flare Wingman in the graveyard meant that Jaden couldn't be harmed by Aster's move. Plus, he now had two new Heroes on the field.

"Looks like your Misfortune has no target," Jaden said. "Oh, well! Good stuff, huh?"

Crowler and Bonaparte looked miserable. They both wanted Aster to beat Jaden. But Jaden had an answer to every one of Aster's tricks!

"Who's the man? I am!" Jaden said confidently. "And here's why, bro. I play Fusion Gate!"

Jaden held up the card. "Now I can fuse monsters *without* Polymerization. And since this is a new field spell card, it cancels out Big Ben over there!"

Jaden grinned, proud of his strategy. With the clock tower gone, Aster's life points could be attacked again.

The stone walls of the prison began to crumble. The whole field shook. The clock tower broke apart and collapsed in an explosion of dust.

"Hey, Aster! Sounds like the bell's tolling for *you* now. So how's it feel?" Jaden called out.

But Aster looked extremely pleased. "Awesome!" he replied. "I was hoping you'd do that."

"You were?" Jaden asked.

"Did you honestly believe I'd let you make a decision on your own?" Aster said. "I wanted this to crumble, to release the monster hiding inside. And now, come on out . . . Destiny Hero - Dreadmaster!"

A huge, hulking figure emerged from the collapsed clock tower. It stood behind Aster, towering over him and his other monsters. A metal mask covered his face. Thick chains were wrapped around his muscled body.

"It won't be much longer now," Aster promised. "Wait till you see what this guy can do. There's a reason why they call him Dreadmaster!"

• CHAPTER TEN •

THE CRUEL HAND OF DESTINY

"When Dreadmaster is summoned, the first thing he does is destroy all my non-Destiny Heroes," Aster explained. "They're not worthy to be in his presence."

Destiny Hero - Dreadmaster raised his fists, and a wicked wind whipped up. Elemental Hero Avian shattered and disappeared from the field.

"That's not all. It gets worse," Aster promised. "Next I can bring back Doom Lord and Captain Tenacious."

The two Destiny Heroes reappeared in front of Aster. He grinned with anticipation.

"Oh yeah," Aster said. "Dreadmaster's attack points are equal to the combined power of every Destiny Hero on the field!"

Dreadmaster grunted as 2800 life points flashed next to him.

"Not bad," Jaden said. "I gotta admit, your monsters get cooler and cooler. But I've got a sweet hero of my own! So let's fuse Clayman and Sparkman to form Elemental Hero Thunder Giant!"

Lightning flashed as Thunder Giant appeared. He wore shining gold armor over his purple uniform. A silver orb on his chest swirled with electric energy. This hero had 2400 attack points.

"And he's got a special effect, too," Jaden continued. "He destroys one of your monsters, as long as its attack points are lower than my Thunder Giant's! So Diamond Dude, you're out of here!"

Jaden pointed at his Hero. "Thunder Giant, activate Static Blast!"

A sizzling lightning bolt shot from the orb on Elemental

Hero Thunder Giant's chest. It zoomed across the field. But before it could strike Destiny Hero - Diamond Dude, Aster held up his hand.

"Sorry, dude!" he told Jaden. "Go, Dread Barrier!"

Dreadmaster pulled off one of the thick chains on his body. He whipped the chain in front of Diamond Dude, blocking Thunder Giant's attack.

Jaden was confused. Why hadn't his attack worked?

"When Dreadmaster is summoned to the field in attack mode, Dread Barrier kicks in," Aster explained. "It protects all Destiny Heroes from damage."

"Great," Jaden said flatly. Aster had a counter for *everything*.

"It's hopeless, man," Aster said. "Listen. Your dueling skills might not be half bad, however, there's something I have that you'll never have. My father was a duelist. He worked as a card designer for Maximillion Pegasus. My dad put his heart into every design he created. He was my hero."

"What happened?" Jaden asked.

A dark look crossed Aster's face.

Suddenly, Jaden realized something. "Did your dad design —"

Aster nodded. "That's right. My father created the Destiny Heroes. They were the last cards he ever made. My father always taught me that there was justice in the world. And in honor of him, I use the very cards he created. That's why I duel." Aster got a faraway look in his eyes.

Jaden felt bad for Aster. His anger was totally controlling him.

"Aster, your dad made those cards so people could use them for fun," Jaden said.

Aster's hands curled into fists. "You don't know anything about him. Butt out!" he said angrily. His voice rose to a shout. "Didn't you hear what I said? He was my hero!"

Aster looked down at his Duel Disk and drew a card. "Where were we? Oh, I remember! We were at the end," he said. "It's been a real blast, Jaden!"

Behind Aster, Destiny Hero - Dreadmaster let out a huge roar.

"Dreadmaster! Send Jaden out with a bang!" Aster cried.

Dreadmaster obeyed. He bounded across the field in a giant leap. Then he pounded Elemental Hero Thunder Giant with a huge fist. The big Hero crumpled in a heap, then disappeared from the field.

Aster grinned. "Oh well. Told ya. You can't hide from Destiny!"

Jaden's life points dropped to zero. His Hero monsters left the field, one by one. In the stands, Jaden's friends gasped in horror.

"Jaden lost!" cried Alexis.

All of Jaden's cards flew out of his Duel Disk. They scattered across the floor of the field.

"His cards!" yelled Syrus and Hassleberry.

Jaden groaned. He felt . . . faint.

"Something doesn't feel right," Jaden moaned.

He collapsed to the floor in a heap.

CHAPTER ELEVEN

A STRANGE PROBLEM

Syrus ran to the medical center at Duel Academy. A crowd of students blocked the doors. They were all talking excitedly.

"Did you hear about Jaden?"

"Yeah, he can't duel anymore!"

Syrus pushed through the crowd.

"Out of the way!" he said crossly.

The automatic doors slid open. The students tumbled into the room in a heap.

"Take a hike, dorks," Chazz told them.

The boys hesitated. They all wanted a glimpse of Jaden.

"I said, beat it!" Chazz yelled.

The boys quickly ran away. Syrus picked himself up and ran into the room. Chazz, Bastion, Alexis, and Hassleberry all stood behind Jaden. He sat in a chair, facing Fontaine. She was supervisor of the girls' Obelisk Blue dorm, as well as the academy's chief medic.

"It's not true, right?" Syrus asked anxiously. "'Cause my lab partner's sister's third cousin said that Jaden can't duel! Please tell me it's just another rumor."

"Nope, it's true," Chazz said. "According to Jaden, he can't see any of his cards!"

Chazz took Jaden's deck from his pocket and handed it to Syrus. Syrus looked through them. He could see them all just fine.

"Huh?" Syrus asked.

"He claims they're all blank," Chazz explained.

"They look fine to *me*. What's the deal?" Syrus asked.

Fontaine finished checking Jaden's eyes. She looked up at Syrus. "The cards aren't the problem," she said. "It's Jaden. During his last duel, something must have happened to him."

Syrus turned to his friend. "Are you messing with us?" he asked.

"Not this time," Jaden said quietly. He stood up. "Oh well. What are you gonna do?"

Jaden turned to walk out of the room. He didn't look at any of his friends.

"Where are you going?" Syrus asked.

"I just need to chill by myself, Sy," Jaden said.

Syrus frowned. Jaden had been through a lot of bad stuff before. Nothing ever got him down. But now Jaden seemed really depressed. It wasn't like Jaden at all.

"Poor guy," Syrus said, watching Jaden go.

Chancellor Crowler also watched Jaden leave the medical center.

"I've never *seen* Jaden like this," he remarked. "Poor lad's devastated. Perhaps I should go talk to him."

Then he realized what he had just said.

"No, no, no!" Crowler cried. "What's happening to me? Could I be turning into a good guy?"

Jaden walked on, leaving Crowler and his friends behind.

He had a lot of thinking to do.

• CHAPTER TWELVE •

ONE FOR ALL

Jaden's friends gathered in the lobby of the Slifer Red dorm. They were all worried about Jaden.

Chazz sat by himself on a bench. The spirit of the Ojama Yellow card flew out of the deck. Chazz had a special connection to the weird looking monster.

"Oh, the horror. The horror!" Ojama Yellow wailed. He had a round yellow body. Two big eyes bobbed on top of long eyestalks. All he wore was a skimpy bathing suit. "Jaden can't talk to his cards anymore! What if it was you, boss?"

The little monster began to sob. He flew around Chazz's head. "I can't go there! It's too — hey!"

Chazz waved Ojama Yellow away with his hand.

"We've got a problem," Bastion said. "This dorm. With Jaden out, they might tear it down."

Syrus nodded. Vice Chancellor Bonaparte wanted nothing more than to see the whole Slifer Red Dorm destroyed. He thought the "Slifer Slackers" were ruining the reputation of the school. Jaden was such a good duelist the dorm had been safe. But if Jaden was really going to quit dueling . . .

"He's right, guys," Syrus said, sighing. "We're doomed."

"Our headquarters? Gone?" Hassleberry couldn't believe it.

"Hmm," Chazz said thoughtfully. "We may be one man down, but we're five men strong."

"Ahem!" Alexis said.

"Well, four men and a lovely lady," Chazz corrected himself. "All right. Three men, a lady, and Syrus. The point is, we gotta fight!"

Chazz stood up and pumped his right fist in the air.

"Here, here, Chazz!" Bastion agreed.

"I'm in," Alexis said.

"I'll stand by and cheer," Syrus joined in.

Hassleberry sprang to his feet. "How about a group 'Yee Hah!'"

Everyone stood up now. They all raised their arms high.

"Yee-Haaaaaaaah!" they yelled.

Hassleberry looked serious. "Crowler, if you try anything, you'll crash into a wall of brotherhood!" he promised.

"Sisterhood, too," Alexis said. "All for one, right guys?"

"And one for all!" Bastion finished.

◆ CHAPTER THIRTEEN ◆

JADEN'S JOURNEY

Jaden would never be sure if the next few days — or was it hours? — had really happened, or if they were a dream. The alien dolphin had said he wasn't dreaming, but still, Jaden couldn't be sure. After all, it *was* an alien dolphin talking to him.

It started when Jaden walked away from Duel Academy. He was in a dark mood. Dueling was his life. It was all he'd ever dreamed of doing since he was a little kid. Coming to Duel Academy had brought him closer to that dream than ever.

And now he couldn't see his cards, when everyone else could. He couldn't explain it.

"I wish things could be like they were last year,"

Jaden muttered to himself. "Back when losing a duel didn't mean losing your mind. What am I supposed to do now?"

Jaden didn't know what to do. So he climbed on a boat and sailed away from the island. It wasn't a very good plan, he knew. But he just wanted to get away.

Hours passed. Jaden leaned back, staring at the night sky.

"How about giving me a sign?" he asked out loud. "Should I give up? Or duel again?"

One of the stars in the sky grew large and bright. It fell from the sky, sailing toward Jaden. As it got closer, Jaden was blinded by its intense light. He could feel its searing heat on his skin.

"*Aaaaaaaaaaaaah!*" Jaden cried.

Everything went black. When Jaden woke up, he felt like he was floating. He opened his eyes. He wasn't in water. He was floating in a sky of swirling, rainbow light.

That's when the dolphin from space had appeared.

It looked like some kind of Duel Monster, Jaden had guessed. But he'd never seen one like it before. The creature stood on two legs, but he had the long, sleek body and face of a dolphin. A dolphin's fin jutted from his blue-skinned back. Four red jewels gleamed on his slick, white chest. He had a long snout, like a dolphin, but he could talk like a human.

That's when things started to get *really* weird.

"You are in Neo Space, Jaden," the creature said. "I am a super-evolved Neo-Spacian Aqua Dolphin. But you may call me Aquos."

"You have a gift," Aquos told him.

Aquos showed Jaden cards that Jaden had designed when he was just a kid. He'd designed the cards for a contest run by Kaiba Corp. Jaden's cards had been made real. Now he could duel again.

The space around Jaden got all swirly. He started to feel funny.

He blacked out.

• CHAPTER FOURTEEN •

FLARE SCARAB

When Jaden woke up, he found himself in the woods of Academy Island. He wasn't sure exactly where he was.

Jaden was tired and hungry. He fell right back to sleep. He dreamed of duels he'd had in his past.

Then he heard a voice in his head.

Jaden. We need you.

Jaden opened his eyes. He saw a column of smoke rising in the distance. He stood up to get a better look. The smoke was coming from a nearby hillside.

"That doesn't look good," he remarked.

Jane walked to the hillside. He saw an opening in the craggy rock and walked inside. A wall of heat greeted him.

Jaden walked a short way through a tunnel; it opened up to reveal a huge pool of bubbling lava.

The bubbling lava rose up into a wave. The wave took shape in front of Jaden's eyes. Then the burning fire faded, and a Duel Monster stood there.

He was a tall monster with gray stone armor over his body. The helmet on top of his head took the curved shape of the horn of an Egyptian beetle.

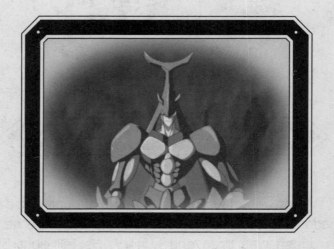

"I'm sorry, but am I supposed to know you?" Jaden asked.

"I am what is known as a Neo-Spacian Flare Scarab," the monster replied in a deep voice. "But call me Flick."

"Did you just say you're a Neo-Spacian?" Jaden asked. "What a coincidence. So's he. Any chance you know Aquos?"

Jaden took his deck of cards from his pocket. The card on top had a picture of Aquos on it — the alien dolphin he'd met.

"Of course," Flick answered. "He's a Water Spacian. I'm a being of fire."

"Are there others?" Jaden wondered.

"Yes, and our forces have converged within your deck," Flick said. He pointed a finger at Jaden's deck. A ray of light shot out and enveloped the deck. Jaden gasped.

"Now follow me and I'll show you more," Flick said.

Flick transformed into a ball of light. He flew out of the lava pool, into the tunnel.

"Cool, but wait up!" Jaden cried.

Jaden emerged from the tunnel out into the moonlight. Flick was gone.

Then Jaden's deck of cards glowed green. Jaden looked through them.

His cards weren't blank anymore! He could see them all.

Well, almost all. One card was still blank.

"Winged Kuriboh," Jaden said sadly. That little card had helped him through some of his most difficult battles. So why couldn't he see it?

Oh! Oh!

Winged Kuriboh's mournful cry suddenly called to Jaden from the woods. Jaden ran as fast as he could toward the sound.

Jaden skidded to a stop in front of a band of rainbow light in the air in front of him. The light twinkled and faded, revealing Winged Kuriboh! The monster flew around Jaden, crying out happily.

"I knew I'd see you again!" Jaden said.

Winged Kuriboh nodded and disappeared into Jaden's deck. Jaden grinned.

He was ready to duel now.

Jaden looked into the distance. The lights were blazing in the school's dueling arena.

Must be some dueling action going on, Jaden guessed. *Might as well get in on it.*

Jaden put his deck in his jacket pocket and headed out into the night.

CHAPTER FIFTEEN

A DUEL FOR THE DORM

Jaden was right. There was a duel brewing in the arena. A duel cooked up by Crowler and Bonaparte.

The two school heads sat in the nearly empty stands. Across from them sat Hasslbery, Bastion, and Syrus.

On the dueling field, Alexis faced off against none other than Aster Phoenix. Even though she was an Obelisk Blue student, Alexis was dueling for the Slifer Red dorm. Aster was dueling for Crowler and Bonaparte.

The stakes were high. If Alexis lost, Bonaparte would get his wish, and the Slifer Red dorm would be demolished.

Bonaparte looked down on the scene with glee. Alexis was good — but Aster was the best in the world. The dorm would be a pile of toothpicks before the sun rose.

The little man stood and cleared his throat. "Attencion!" he said in his bad French accent. "Should Alexis lose this duel, it's au revoir, Red dorm!"

"Not gonna happen, folks!" Alexis said firmly.

Aster grinned.

"Get your game on!" he taunted.

A familiar voice rang across the arena.

"Hey, that's my line!"

Everyone looked shocked as Jaden ran into the arena.

"It's Jaden!" Syrus cried.

"Hey guys," Jaden said. He stopped to catch his breath. "Did everybody miss me? 'Cause I've gone where no man has gone before!"

"Couldn't you have just stayed there?" Aster grumbled.

"Of course not," Jaden said. "There wasn't any oxygen there, and besides, they didn't get cable."

Everyone stared at Jaden, confused.

"See, I went to outer space," Jaden explained. "And I chilled with this dolphin man. He gave me these totally rad cards for my deck!"

Bastion shook his head. "Poor guy's gone mad."

"Wow, I've always wanted to hang with an alien!" Syrus said.

"Trust me, it gets weirder," Jaden said. He told the story of meeting Flick, and being able to see his cards again.

"So my deck's even sweeter now!" Jaden bragged.

Syrus sighed. "All the cool stuff happens to him."

Jaden called across the field. "Aster! How'd you like the honor of being the first duelist to lose to my new deck? 'Cause I got a rockin' set of heroes now, and they're ready to throw down!"

Aster sneered. "Will you listen to yourself? You're insane! There's not a hero monster on Earth that can hold a candle to mine!"

"Weren't you listening?" Jaden asked. "My heroes came from outer space, not Earth!"

Jaden turned to Alexis. "Let me take your place. I need to do this!"

Jaden didn't wait for an answer. He jumped up onto the dueling field.

"You won't regret this, Alexis!" he said.

Bonaparte scowled. "That's not fair!"

"Sure it is!" Bastion shot back. "Jaden lives in the Slifer Red dorm as well. So he has just as much of a right to fight for it."

Chancellor Crowler stepped in. He had a soft spot

for the Slifer Red dorm that he couldn't quite explain. But if Jaden had a chance to save it, Crowler was going to give it to him.

"Very well," he said, as Bonaparte fumed beside him. "I suppose we can make an exception this time."

"Thanks a mil, Chancellor Crowler!" Jaden called out. "You don't know how much I've missed dueling!"

"Do you miss *losing*?" Aster asked.

Alexis threw Jaden her Duel Disk.

"Go get him!" she yelled.

"Hey, thanks. I owe you," Jaden replied.

Crowler stood up. "All right, that's enough! On with the duel!"

• CHAPTER SIXTEEN •

THE DEBUT OF NEOS

"Game on!" Jaden cried.

Both duelists activated their Duel Disks. They each started the duel with 4000 life points.

"I'll kick things off first," Aster said. "And who better to start the hurt than my Diamond Dude?"

Aster's monster appeared on the field, his sharp spikes gleaming. Fourteen hundred attack points flashed next to him.

"And now for a little special effect action!" Aster said. "First I draw the top card on my deck! And it happens to be a spell card. It automatically activates on my next turn."

Aster held up the card. It showed an angelic creature with her hands held out.

"Now for the moment of truth. It's the spell card Graceful Charity!" he cried triumphantly. "I love it when a plan comes together."

"So do I," Jaden said. "And here's mine. You're not the only one who can start with a hero. And believe me, this one is guaranteed to make a splash. So meet Neo-Spacian Aqua Dolphin!"

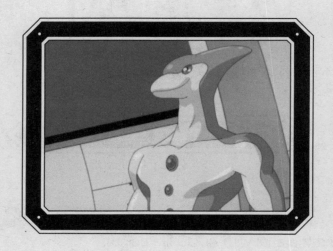

A huge wave of water rose up behind Jaden as Aquos appeared on the field. Everyone gasped at the sight of the strange monster.

"It's true!" Bastion exclaimed. "Jaden's heroes *are* aliens."

Jaden was pleased with the reaction. "Next I activate my Fake Hero spell card," he said. He held up the card. "Here's how it works. Now I'm able to summon one monster from my hand. But it returns to my hand when the turn's over. Now come on out, Elemental Hero Bladedge!"

Bladedge appeared on the field, a shining monster with bright gold armor over every inch of his body. He boasted a serious 2600 attack points.

"And since Aqua Dolphin's special ability is in the house, I can ditch one card from my hand in order to grab a monster from yours," Jaden announced.

Aster looked horrified as Jaden put a card in his graveyard. Neo-Spacian Aqua Dolphin opened his mouth and a powerful blast of sonar poured out. The sonar targeted one of the cards in Aster's hand. As it shone on the card, Destiny Hero - Captain Tenacious appeared — and then immediately vanished into the graveyard.

"Not him!" Aster cried.

"Next I pick a monster on my side," Jaden explained. "And if mine happens to be stronger, then yours goes bye-bye! And one more thing. You lose five hundred life points!"

Aster covered his face with his hands as he was hit with a wild blast. His life points dropped down to 3500.

"Not bad, huh?" Jaden asked. "Next I'll throw these down, take back Bladedge, and chill out!"

Jaden put two cards facedown on the field. Elemental Hero Bladedge vanished. Then Jaden faced Aster, waiting for him to make his move.

"Lucky shot," Aster said, his eyes blazing with determination. "But now it's my move! Time for Graceful Charity. I draw three cards, and then I get rid of two."

Aster examined the cards he had drawn. He smiled and chose the one he wanted.

"Now pay attention class," Aster said snidely. "Ready? I activate a spell card . . . Mausoleum of the Emperor!"

Aster placed the card on his Duel Disk, and a gray fog rose up on the field. The spell began to transform the duel arena into an ancient-looking tomb with stone walls and towers. Jaden glanced around and saw what looked like an army of stone soldiers filling the space below them.

"Just to make this place even creepier, the basement's filled with a bunch of old statues," Aster explained. "We can both use them. All we have to do is give up some points. Then we can sacrifice these statues to summon monsters!"

As Aster spoke, his life points dropped from 3500 to 2500 points. Two stone soldiers rose into the air, then vanished. Aster had sacrificed them.

He triumphantly raised his arm. "Now I'll call to the field my Destiny Hero - Dreadmaster!"

Aster's gigantic hero appeared, groaning behind his metal mask.

"And now that the Master of Dread is here, I can bring two heroes back from the grave!" Aster announced. "So without further ado, I summon Captain Tenacious and Doom Lord!"

Creepy-looking Destiny Hero - Doom Lord materialized with his 600 attack points. Red-haired Destiny Hero - Captain Tenacious stood next to him, 800 attack points strong.

"Their combined power gets added to my Dreadmaster's attack points!" Aster bragged. The monster's attack points rose to 2800.

Aster pointed at Aquos. "You ready, Dolphin Boy? Let's see what kind of tricks you can do! Dreadmaster, turn Flipper into fish sticks!"

Dreadmaster raised a massive fist in front of him and flew across the field.

"Hold it, muscle-head!" Jaden yelled. A trap card in front of him flipped up. "Negate Attack!"

A tornado of light spiraled out from the card, pushing Destiny Hero - Dreadmaster back to Aster.

"Thanks to this, your attack is over even before it began," Jaden notified him. "That's all she wrote, pal."

"I'm not your pal!" Aster snapped angrily.

Jaden shrugged. "Just trying to be nice," he said. "Anyway, thanks in advance for sharing your spell card with me."

Jaden gave up 1000 life points, bringing his total to 3000. He sacrificed two stone soldiers.

"Now I can summon him . . . my Elemental Hero Neos!"

Aster scowled. "There's no such thing, dude. Trust me. I know every hero there is."

But Aster was quickly proven wrong. A hero in a silver uniform flew onto the field. Two alien-like eyes stared from the mask on his face. Neos boasted an impressive 2500 attack points.

"Well, fine. But I bet he's totally lame," Aster said. "So let's see what you got, space man! Zap me with your ray gun."

"He doesn't have one," Jaden said. "But he does have a pretty cool trick. You see, Neo-Spacians like to work together. When these two are both on the field I can fuse them into a new hero. Aqua and Neos, merge together, in order to form Elemental Hero Aqua Neos!"

The two Neo Heroes flew over the field. A bright light engulfed them, and when it vanished, a new hero stood next to Jaden. Aqua Neos had the sleek, silver body of Neos and the blue back fin of Aquos. A sharp, blue fin spiked up on the monster's head, and blue fins jutted from each of his muscled arms. The new monster had 2500 attack points.

"Wait'll you see what he can do!" Jaden said. "If I get rid of one of my cards, two random cards in your deck are destroyed. So I'll toss out my Elemental Hero Bladedge."

Jaden sent his monster to the graveyard. Then light rays shot out of Aqua Neos's eyes. They zapped two of Aster's cards, destroying them. Aster cried out in surprise.

"Next I activate Heated Heart," Jaden said, as the card flipped up in front of him. "Thanks to this, my Aqua Neos gets stronger by five hundred points!"

Aqua Neos's attack points climbed to 3000.

"Aqua Neos, attack!" Jaden ordered. "Destroy his Dreadmaster with Sonic Zoom!"

Aqua Neos raised both arms in the air, raising energy for the attack. He lowered his arms and hurled a massive blast of sonic energy at Destiny Hero - Dreadmaster.

Boom! The huge hero shattered and left the field. Aster cringed as his own life points dropped down to 2300.

"Gotcha!" Jaden cheered.

"Your Martian Mutant is nothing next to my Destiny Heroes!" Aster yelled angrily.

"Really?" Jaden asked. "Cause I coulda sworn—"

He stopped. Elemental Hero Aqua Neos was turning into rainbow light right in front of him. The light poured itself into Jaden's Duel Disk!

"Hello?" Jaden called. "Excuse me, Mr. Neos? We're kinda in the middle of something here!"

Jaden's friends in the stands reacted with concern.

"If you fellows ask me, I'd say he has a lot to learn about his new deck," Bastion said.

Syrus was worried. "Jaden's wide open now!"

Aster was obviously aware of that fact. His angry mood had changed.

"Since you're fresh out of monsters I'll assume you're done," he said. "So now I'll show you what *real* heroes can do. And the best way to do that is with this — a triple attack!"

Aster pointed at his three monsters. "Diamond Dude, Captain Tenacious, and Doom Lord, let's do this. Direct attack!"

Jaden braced himself. With no monster to protect him, he'd take every hit directly!

Whack! Bam! Wham! The monsters slammed into Jaden one by one. His life points plummeted down to 200! Jaden tumbled to the floor, groaning.

"Jaden!" Syrus cried.

Aster grinned. "Soon you'll lose your life points. Then you'll lose your dorm!"

◆ CHAPTER SEVENTEEN ◆

HUMMINGBIRD HELPS OUT

Jaden climbed to his feet. "Come on, bro. I was just getting warmed up. Now the *real* duel can start!"

Jaden loved being in a tight spot and trying to figure his way out. To him, that was one of the best parts of dueling. Pure energy was flowing through his body now, and he loved the feeling.

Still, he had some thinking to do.

I guess I've got a lot to learn about my new deck, Jaden realized. *For one, Aqua Neos has a serious weakness. He only sticks around for one turn. Wish I knew that a few minutes ago.*

"All right. Enough thinking!" Jaden said out loud. He held out a card. "It's time for some action! So I play Elemental Hero Bubbleman!"

Jaden's blue hero appeared on the field with 800 attack points.

"And get this!" Jaden continued. "Since he's the only card in my hand, Bubbleman counts as a special summon. *And*, since he's alone on the field, I'm allowed to draw two cards!"

Jaden looked at his new cards and smiled.

"Awesome! I just drew Pot of Greed, so I pick two more cards!" Jaden cried. He took the cards. "And one of them's Bubble Blaster! Go, me!"

Jaden couldn't believe his luck. Bubble Blaster was a great card to draw when Elemental Hero Bubbleman was on the field.

"Now my Bubbleman gets eight hundred extra points!" Jaden said happily, as the hero's attack points rose to 1600. The huge Bubble Blaster weapon appeared on Bubbleman's right arm, ready for action.

And Jaden had another card to be happy about, too. "And now I'd like to introduce a surprise guest. Making his debut here on planet Earth, it's Neo-Spacian Air Hummingbird!"

Jaden put the card in his Duel Disk. A bright green light shot out and flew high overhead. The light swooped back down and landed on the field in front of Jaden. The ball of light burst, revealing a new Neo hero.

Air Hummingbird stood tall on two legs. His body was covered with red feathers, and his head looked like a bird's head with a long, yellow beak. Two strong, white wings stretched out on his back. The hero had 800 attack points.

Neo-Spacian Air Hummingbird turned and looked at Jaden.

A wise move, Jaden, he said, his words reaching directly into Jaden's mind. *Now let us win.*

Jaden nodded. "All right, Hummingbird, now do your thing. Honey Suck!"

Air Hummingbird flew across the field. The three cards in Aster's hands began to glow with white light. Aster gasped as they transformed into three large flowers.

Air Hummingbird stuck his beak into each flower and began to suck out the nectar there.

"I know it looks weird, but it's actually a pretty rad special ability," Jaden explained. "For each card in your hand, my Hummingbird sucks out five hundred points — and I get them!"

Jaden grinned as his life points rose to 1700.

"It'll take more than that," Aster said.

"I know," Jaden said cheerfully. "Like this guy — Bubbleman!"

Elemental Hero Bubbleman aimed the Bubble Blaster

at Captain Tenacious. A torrent of water shot across the field.

Wham! The attack washed out the red-headed hero.

Aster frowned. His life points dropped to 1500.

"And remember, my Hummingbird didn't attack yet," Jaden said. "Well, until now. Slaughtering Swoop!"

Air Hummingbird flew up into the air, then dove right at Destiny Hero - Doom Lord!

Bam! He slammed into the creepy hero, sending him to the graveyard. Aster's life points dropped down to 1300.

Next Jaden threw down a facedown card, ending his turn.

His friends were impressed.

"What a comeback!" Alexis said. "Jaden almost lost, and now he's actually winning!"

Bastion nodded. "That's Jaden. He's got a flair for the dramatic, wouldn't you say?"

But Aster was mostly annoyed. "I've had enough of your lame space cadets," he sneered. "I prefer to duel in the real world. So now I activate the field spell card, Dark City!"

The ancient tomb vanished from the field, and dark city skyscrapers rose up to replace it. A bright moon hung in the night sky overhead, casting spooky shadows over everything.

"A little change of scenery never hurt, right?" Aster asked. "Now if a Destiny Hero's weaker than the opposing monster, it gains a thousand attack points!"

Even Jaden had to admit that was a good move.

"Pretty sweet card, Aster," he said. "Nicely played."

"There's more," Aster promised. "I'm ditching Diamond Dude to summon this — Destiny Hero - Double Dude!"

Diamond Dude disappeared into the graveyard. The new hero Aster produced definitely looked sinister. Destiny Hero - Double Dude was a thin man in a black suit and hat. He wore a black scarf over his nose and mouth. Empty eyes gazed from his pale face. He held a long, black cane. Double Dude had 1000 attack points, but they jumped to 2000, thanks to the powers of Dark City.

"Attack Bubbleman!" Aster commanded. "Burst his bubble!"

Jaden stepped forward. "Did you forget? Instead of my Bubbleman going boom, his Blaster does!"

Destiny Hero - Double Dude flew across the field. He

transformed into a savage-looking hero with wild gray hair. His new, muscled body had burst through his suit.

Like Dr. Jekyll and Mr. Hyde, Jaden thought.

The savage Double Dude pounded the Bubble Blaster, which burst into pieces.

"You forgot — my Double Dude gets a double attack!" Aster said. "So here's round two — bye-bye, birdie!"

Double Dude transformed back into the sinister man in black. He struck Hummingbird with his cane, sending him to the graveyard in one blow.

"Hummingbird!" Jaden wailed. His life points dropped to 1500.

"I'll toss this facedown and give you a break," Aster said, ending his turn.

"Not bad, but check this out," Jaden said, holding up a card. "It's my Graceful Charity. So I'll pick up three and toss out two."

Jaden took the cards and chose the one he wanted.

"Now I'll reveal Disgraceful Charity," he said. The new card floated in front of him. "Here's the deal. For this round only, any cards we happen to discard come back to our hands."

Jaden put another card in his Duel Disk.

"Next I'll play Common Soul," he said. The card showed a picture of some kind of Neo-Spacian. "Thanks to this little spell card, I can summon my Neo-Spacian hero, Flare Scarab!"

Jaden's friend Flick appeared on the field, with 500 attack points.

"Another one of your alien friends?" Aster asked.

"You betcha," Jaden replied. "And you're right. These guys are my friends. In fact, I didn't find them. These heroes found me! I mean, how cool is that?"

Aster shook his head in disgust. "You're nuts!" he cried. "You duel in a fantasy world. Well, it's about time you grew up. I duel by using the power of Destiny — and I never lose!"

CHAPTER EIGHTEEN

BATTLE OF THE HEROES

"You're forgetting the most important thing," Jaden shouted back. "Dueling is about making friends and having a blast, isn't it? That's why your father started designing the cards in the first place!"

Jaden's words struck Aster like an arrow. Memories flooded back to Aster . . . memories of his dad, smiling and laughing with Aster as he worked on designing new cards.

Jaden's right, Aster realized. *My father created the Destiny Heroes to make me happy! What would he think of me now? Every time I use the Destiny Heroes, all I feel is pain. What happened to me?*

Aster stood frozen on the field, not moving. Jaden wanted to make his move, but he patiently waited for Aster to gather his thoughts.

Bonaparte wasn't happy.

"Do something!" he pleaded with Crowler. "You're supposed to be in charge of this school!"

But down below, something important was happening to Aster.

I should be using my Heroes for good! Aster thought.

"Back to the duel!" Jaden called out.

Aster snapped out of his thoughts. He might have seen the light — but that didn't mean he still didn't want to beat Jaden. He'd just have to wait until Jaden's turn was over.

"Flare Scarab, you're up, pal," Jaden said. "Activate Smolder Serge!"

Flames burst from Neo-Spacian Flare Scarab's body.

"Here's how it works," Jaden said. "For every trap and spell card on your side of the field, my Flare Scarab gains four hundred attack points."

Flare Scarab roared as the flames leapt higher, while his attack points jumped to a scorching 1300.

"And next, thanks to my Common Soul, Flare Scarab is able to help out one of his peeps by sharing his attack points!" Jaden said.

A stream of light shot from Flare Scarab's body. Elemental Hero Bubbleman cried out as the light flowed into him, bringing his attack points to 2100.

"Now, Bubbleman, take down his Double Dude!" Jaden ordered.

Elemental Hero Bubbleman flew up, his cape flapping in the air behind him. He blasted Destiny Hero - Double Dude with a powerful jet of water. The sinister hero vanished into the graveyard, and Aster's life points dropped all the way down to 200.

"No biggie," Aster said. "I'll just play this! Destiny Signal!"

Aster used the spell card to summon a Destiny Hero from his deck.

"Destiny Hero - Defender!" he cried.

Defender looked like a big, bulky robot made up of metal blocks. Red eyes glowed from behind a small cage in his metal head. True to his name, he was a defensive pow-erhouse with 2700 defense points.

"Not bad," Jaden remarked. "That's a whole lotta defense points for one hero."

"Told you!" Aster shot back. "My Destiny Heroes are the coolest cards in the game. And you haven't even seen them all yet. But, uh, thanks for the props, I guess."

Now it was Aster's turn to make a move.

"Since you destroyed my Double Dude, its special

ability activates!" Aster said. "When it goes to the grave-yard, two Double Dude Tokens show up on the field to take his place!"

Two heroes that looked just like Double Dude appeared on the field. They each had 1000 attack points.

Aster held up another card. "Next I play Mystical Space Typhoon!" he cried. A strong wind whipped out from the card. "Nice weather we're having, isn't it? But your space man might not agree."

Jaden watched as the wind destroyed Neo-Spacian Flare Scarab. The quick-spell card had done its work.

"But I loved that guy!" Jaden protested.

"Don't forget, without him, your Bubbleman gets weaker," Aster pointed out.

Jaden gasped in shock as Bubbleman's attack points dropped back to 800.

"Go, Token One!" Aster ordered.

The Doom Lord Token raced across the field and smashed Elemental Hero Bubbleman with his cane. Bubbleman shattered, and Jaden's life points dropped down to 1300.

"Now, Token Number Two!" Aster yelled.

Jaden didn't have time to react. The other Doom Lord swooped down from the sky, attacking him directly. When the smoke cleared, he only had 300 life points left. Jaden groaned.

But he wasn't down yet.

"Thanks to your Defender, I can draw two cards instead of one," Jaden remembered. He drew the two new cards. "I'll start with Shallow Grave!"

He put the spell card into his Duel Disk.

"Now we each pick a monster from our graveyard and bring him back to the field, but they have to be in defense mode," Jaden explained. "So I choose my Hero Kid!"

But this hero didn't look like it could defend very much. Hero Kid looked like a small boy. He wore a red, yellow, and black uniform. A red mask covered his eyes, and a clear bubble of defense protected his head. He had 600 defense points.

"And when this kid is special-summoned, two more little heroes can join him," Jaden said. "So now it's time for a triple threat!"

The other two Hero Kids flashed onto the field. Aster laughed mockingly.

"Come on. Do you honestly think those little brats have a shot against my Destiny Heroes?" he jeered. "Like Dreadmaster?"

Aster's biggest hero returned from the graveyard. He got into defense position behind Aster.

"And when this big guy's here, all of my non-Destiny Heroes run for cover," Aster said. The two Doom Lord tokens shattered. That was the price of playing Destiny Hero - Dreadmaster.

"But of course they get replaced with two new heroes," Aster said. "Like my Diamond Dude and Captain Tenacious!"

The two Destiny Heroes came back to the field in defense mode. Diamond Dude had 1600 defense points, and Tenacious had 800.

"And Dreadmaster's defense points are equal to the sum of the attack points of Diamond Dude and Captain Tenacious!" Aster said. He smiled confidently as Dreadmaster's 2300 defense points flashed on the field.

Jaden wasn't worried. "What a coincidence," he said. "I'm about to bring back an old friend also. My Flare Scarab! And thanks to Dark City, he gets points, too!"

Neo-Spacian Flare Scarab appeared on the field once more, and his 500 attack points jumped to 900.

"Flare Scarab, attack his Captain now!" Jaden ordered.

The Neo hero's body burned with flame. A blast of fire shot from his body and slammed into Destiny Hero - Captain Tenacious. The hero vanished once again, and Dreadmaster's defense points dropped down as a result.

Jaden threw down two facedowns to end his turn.

"That's it?" Aster asked. "How lame! Watch the pro."

Aster held up a card. "Pot of Greed! I pick up two cards and sacrifice Dreadmaster, plus my Defender and Diamond Dude!"

Jaden was surprised. Why was Aster sacrificing all his monsters? There had to be a big payoff.

Jaden was right.

"Now I can play my Destiny Hero - Dogma!" he cried.

A massive monster appeared in the night sky. Dogma had huge black wings, black armor, and a sharp tail like a scorpion. He looked scary, and his attack points were even scarier — 3400!

"Now that's what I call a monster!" Jaden said.

His friends were all shocked.

"Great Scott!" said Bastion.

"Aw, man!" Syrus whined.

"Sam Hill!" Hassleberry exclaimed.

Why don't I have a catch phrase? Alexis wondered.

Aster paused dramatically. With this move, he'd easily win the duel.

"Now, Dogma!" he yelled. "Attack his Flare Scarab!"

◆ CHAPTER NINETEEN ◆

WELCOME TO NEO SPACE

Purple light flared from Destiny Hero - Dogma. He raced across the field, ready to deliver Jaden's doom.

Jaden grinned and pointed at Aster.

"You triggered my trap!" he cried. Jaden's trap card flipped up. It had a picture of Hero Kid on it. "Kid Guard! Thanks to this, I can sacrifice one of my Hero Kids in order to cancel your attack. Then I can grab an Elemental Hero card from anywhere inside my deck!"

One of the Hero Kids nodded to Jaden. He bravely faced Dogma. The purple light shattered Hero Kid's protective shield, and the young hero vanished.

Then Jaden heard Flare Scarab's voice in his head.

Jaden! You must harness the power of Neos!

Jaden looked down at his deck. He wasn't an expert with his Neo Heroes yet. Should he chance it?

He knew Neo-Spacian Flare Scarab wouldn't steer him wrong.

"I choose my Elemental Hero Neos to end my hand!" Jaden announced.

"Well, I'll drop a facedown and end my turn," Aster countered.

"Remember, for every facedown card you play, my Flared Scarab gets stronger," Jaden said. He watched, pleased, as Scarab's attack points jumped to 1300.

Jaden was ready to make his move. "All right. Go time!"

But Aster had other ideas.

"Not so fast. Go, Dogma!"

The dark hero glowed with purple light once again. Jaden felt his own body heat up as the purple light struck him directly.

"Dogma's special ability cuts your life points in half every standby phase," Aster said smugly.

Jaden only had 150 life points left. Things didn't look good.

"One hit, and it's all over!" Bastion cried.

Jaden laughed. "Not bad! But I got some fight left in me."

"Come on," Aster said. "There's not a card in your deck that can save you."

"Well, maybe not in my old deck, but this deck's another story," Jaden said. "I've got a new hero that nobody's even seen before! But first I play a field spell, Neo Space!"

Aster cried out as his field spell shattered around him. "My Dark City!"

Now the entire field looked like it was floating in space. An aura of rainbow light swirled around everyone.

"This card increases the power of my Elemental Hero Neos by five hundred!" Jaden said.

Neos flew down from the sky. His life points rose from 2500 to 3000.

"So what?" Aster shot back. "It still doesn't stand up to my Dogma!"

"Not yet," Jaden said. "But who said I was done? I'm creating a new monster by combining these two together!"

"That's against the rules!" Aster cried.

"It's called contact fusion and it's legit," Jaden said. "You see, Neo-Spacians can merge without a Polymerization card!"

Flare Scarab and Neos flew up into the swirling lights

of space. The new hero wore gray and red armor. He had two huge orange wings on his back, and an orange and black mask that covered everything on his face except for his green eyes.

Aster thought he'd easily beat Jaden. Now Jaden was pulling out some sweet moves. But instead of feeling annoyed, Aster found he was enjoying it.

I remember this feeling, he thought. *It's like years back, when I was a kid, and dueling was still fun!*

"Meet Elemental Flare Neos!" Jaden called out. "And guess what? He gains 400 attack points for every spell and trap on the field! There are three cards on the field, plus the one I just played, so that gives him 1600 extra points!"

Jaden's hero now boasted an amazing 4200 attack points!

"That's enough to beat my Dogma," Aster realized.

"That's the whole point!" Jaden countered. "Flare Neos, attack!"

Elemental Hero Flare Neos transformed into a scorching wall of flame. The fire swept across the field, ready to destroy Dogma.

"I activate D-Shield!" Aster yelled. His facedown card flipped up, and a white glowing light surrounded Dogma.

"What's that?" Jaden asked.

"It's a trap card," Aster replied. "Now when a Destiny Hero's attacked, it switches to defense mode. *And* it stays on the field!"

Flare Neos flew back to Jaden. He couldn't attack Dogma now.

"Awesome," Jaden said. "Pretty sweet trap, for real!"

"Thank you," Aster answered. "But you know, flattery's not going to get you anywhere. Stand back! I'm guessing that your Neo Space field card keeps your monster from vanishing again."

"That's right!" Jaden answered. "As long as this card's in play, even though he's fused with something else, Neos will be sticking around this time."

Aster grinned. "Not quite," he said. "First things first. I switch Dogma to attack mode, so stand up!"

Destiny Hero - Dogma got back into attack position, his 3400 attack points ready to strike.

"Then I'll equip him with this spell card," Aster said. "Heavy Storm Blade!"

Three sharp blades appeared at the end of Dogma's right hand. They looked almost like a windmill.

Jaden wasn't worried. Aster had used a new spell card — which meant that Flare Neos now had 4600 attack points. Dogma still only had 3400.

"Now attack!" Aster told his Dogma.

Jaden was confused — and so was everyone else.

"That's weird," Syrus said.

"Aster's monster is weaker than Jaden's," Bastion said.

"Well then why would he engage him?" Bastion wondered.

"Excellent question," Aster shouted. "And I can answer it with just four words — my Heavy Storm Blade! Now see for yourselves!"

Dogma flew up above the field. The storm blades spun furiously, creating a strong wind. The wind reached out to both sides of the field.

"Whenever a monster with a Heavy Storm Blade attacks, every single trap and spell card on the field is instantly destroyed!" Aster cried.

Jaden was stunned. "No way!"

The wind slammed into all of the trap and spell cards, blowing them off the field. The swirling lights of Neo Space faded. Now the field was back to normal.

Without Neo Space, Jaden was in trouble. Elemental Hero Flare Neos lost hundreds of life points. They dropped down to 2900 — not enough to withstand Dogma's punishment.

"Now attack!" Aster yelled.

CHAPTER TWENTY

MORE POWERFUL THAN DESTINY

The powerful Storm Blades whirled as Destiny Hero - Dogma flew across the field to destroy Elemental Hero Flare Neos. The two heroes clashed, but Dogma's blades did no damage at all. They broke into pieces.

"No fair!" Aster screamed. *Why was Flare Neos still standing?*

"Maybe," Jaden said, his brown eyes twinkling. He held up a card. "See this? You sent it to my graveyard. And when Spell Calling leaves the field, I get to replace it with two new spell cards. I gave my Neos a power boost!"

Aster couldn't believe his eyes. Elemental Hero Flare Neos had 3700 attack points — 300 more than Dogma.

Impossible! Aster thought. That means Jaden wins.

Destiny Hero - Dogma began to spark and crumble. The hero monster vanished from the field. Aster took the rest of the damage — and lost all the rest of his life points. He cringed and fell to his knees.

"That's game!" Jaden said. "And a sweet one, too." Jaden's friends jumped to their feet.

"He won!" Syrus cheered. "Way to play!"

"Well done, soldier," Hassleberry called out.

"And thanks to Jaden, the dorm is safe now," Alexis added.

Jaden waved to his friends. Aster walked up to him.

"Jaden, I don't say this much, but I'm impressed," he said humbly.

Aster frowned. "Now look, I don't intend to lose again. So you'd better enjoy this moment while it lasts."

Jaden grinned. "Of course, I'm going to milk this victory for all it's worth! I mean, come on. It's not every day that I beat the pants off an undefeated pro duelist. Now here's how I see it . . ."

Aster sighed. He never thought he'd be in a position to let Jaden call the shots.

"We don't count our first duel, since you let me win," Jaden said. "So that means we're tied."

"Yeah?" Aster asked. "Well, not for much longer."

Jaden's friends joined them on the field. They gathered around him, admiring his new cards.

Jaden felt great. He was back. He was dueling again. He had a bunch of new cards on his team — new friends to help him with whatever duels he had to face in the future. He knew he'd face Aster again. And the Neo-Spacians needed him to help restore balance to the universe. But he'd have time to prepare for that later.

Right now, he just wanted to ride the thrill of the duel.